Sometimes When I'm Bored

Deborah Serani, Psy.D.
illustrated by Kyra Teis

free spirit
PUBLISHING®

Library of Congress Cataloging-in-Publication Data
Names: Serani, Deborah, 1961– author. | Teis, Kyra, illustrator.
Title: Sometimes when I'm bored / by Deborah Serani, Psy.D. ; illustrated by Kyra Teis.
Description: Minneapolis, MN : Free Spirit Publishing, [2022] | Series: Sometimes when | Audience: Ages 4–8
Identifiers: LCCN 2021035747 (print) | LCCN 2021035748 (ebook) | ISBN 9781631986956 (hardcover) |
    ISBN 9781631986963 (pdf) | ISBN 9781631986970 (epub)
Subjects: LCSH: Boredom—Juvenile literature.
Classification: LCC BF575.B67 S47 2022 (print) | LCC BF575.B67 (ebook) | DDC 152.4—dc23/eng/20211108
LC record available at https://lccn.loc.gov/2021035747
LC ebook record available at https://lccn.loc.gov/2021035748

Free Spirit Publishing does not have control over or assume responsibility for author or third-party websites and their content.

Reading Level Grade 2; Interest Level Ages 4–8;
Fountas & Pinnell Guided Reading Level K

Edited by Alison Behnke
Cover and interior design by Emily Dyer

10 9 8 7 6 5 4 3 2 1
Printed in China
R18860122

Free Spirit Publishing Inc.
6325 Sandburg Road, Suite 100
Minneapolis, MN 55427-3674
(612) 338-2068
help4kids@freespirit.com
freespirit.com

FSC
www.fsc.org
MIX
Paper from
responsible sources
FSC® C144853

Free Spirit offers competitive pricing.
Contact edsales@freespirit.com for pricing information on multiple quantity purchases.

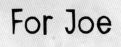

For Joe

Sometimes when I'm bored,
nothing feels fun.

I can't find anything to do.

Sometimes I just stare out the window.

Sometimes when I'm bored,
everything bothers me.

I don't like any of my toys.
I've read all my books.

There's no one to play with.
And I feel lonely.

Sometimes when I'm bored, I feel tired.

Other times, I just feel blah.

Everything is the same. Ugh!

"Momma, I'm bored," I said.

"Well, what a wonderful thing to be!" she said. "When you're bored, something special is waiting for you."

"How do I find it?"

"By trying something new.
Or by asking questions about things
that make you curious," Momma said.

Momma said that when I'm bored
I can also use my imagination,
sing a song, or build things.

"Wondering can help take away feeling bored," Momma said. "What do you wonder?"

"I wonder where those birds are flying," I said. "Do you think there's a nest nearby? Maybe there are baby birds in it."

"Daddy, I'm bored," I said.
"There's no one to play with!"

"Playing pretend can help when you're feeling lonely," Daddy said.

"So can drawing a picture or writing a letter to someone."

"Sometimes I feel so sleepy
when I'm bored," I said.

"You could listen to music or read," Daddy said. "Or you can rest for a few minutes. Sometimes our bodies need a little quiet time."

Daddy said that after I rest, my mind and body may be ready to do something fun.

"What about when everything is the same?" I said.

"That's when you try something new," Daddy said.

"When you do something different," said Momma.

Now when I'm bored and I can't think of anything to do . . .

I get curious about
things around me.

When I'm bored and
nothing feels fun ...

I use my imagination.

When I'm bored and everything feels blah . . .

I do new things.

When I'm bored and I feel lonely . . .

I make a beautiful painting
for my grandma, or write
my best friend a letter.

Now when I'm bored, I know something special is waiting for me.

I just have to find it.

HELPING CHILDREN THROUGH BOREDOM
A Guide for Caring Adults

There are many ways to define or describe boredom: *dullness*, *tedium*, *idleness*, *the ho-hums*, *the blahs*, *doldrums*, *monotony*—and my favorite, the French word *ennui*. When it comes to boredom in children, I believe it's best defined as "a state of dissatisfaction that arises from an inability to find a more meaningful activity." Children who feel bored typically know, deep down, that there are many fun and interesting things to do. But when they are in the grip of boredom, they cannot seem to find *how* to seek out those activities or experiences. This is when the all-too-familiar complaint "I'm bored" is expressed, and children beg the adults in their lives to fix things so the boredom disappears.

Many young children are raised in home and school environments that revolve around structure. They may also spend downtime playing on computers, devices, and other digital platforms. Screen time and scheduled activities can help teach children the value of having routines and go-to playtime tools. However, when little ones are confronted with the timeless experience of just *being*, or just doing nothing, they can feel lost, frustrated, or uneasy. Screen time and overscheduling may appear to be boredom-busters, but, in truth, they are often diversions. And while these activities are meaningful, children also need time on their own to learn more about their own interests, creative urges, and self-care.

Sometimes When I'm Bored teaches children and adults to recognize the textures and effects of boredom. The book also shows readers that the discomfort of boredom can be an invitation to discover something meaningful about themselves—and about the world around them. Learning how to redirect feelings of boredom deepens problem-solving skills and builds the ability to shift negative thoughts to more positive ones.

WHY DOES BOREDOM HAPPEN?

When young children struggle with feeling bored, they are also typically struggling with managing *time*, developing *control*, and building *skills*. Addressing these areas will help them move from boredom to more meaningful experiences.

- **Time:** As many children have highly scheduled lives, when there are breaks to do other, *unplanned* things, little ones can feel uncertain about time management. This is why it's important for adults to provide free time and unstructured play for children. Doing so enables children to become comfortable with unstructured time and gives them the chance to start developing the skills needed to avoid intense boredom. Through this practice, children find the freedom to self-reflect, explore, create, and discover without predetermined rules or guidelines. Unstructured time has been shown to foster cognitive development, imagination, and creativity, as well as boost physical and social development in children.

- **Control:** One of the developmental goals of childhood is to cultivate control, also called agency: the ability to make choices, problem solve, and regulate feelings. Children who feel bored often don't recognize how to set their thoughts or ideas into motion, or how to consider and make choices. When children learn more about their own ability to think, feel, plan, and decide, they develop agency, which in turn helps them take steps to counteract boredom. Children not only feel more in control of their lives, but also gain a sense of belonging and self-confidence. Adults can also encourage autonomy in children to further foster agency. This means allowing children to choose *what* they want to learn and *how* they want to gain that knowledge. Another tip is to inspire a child to make *learning* the goal instead of *achievement*. In this way, little ones come to love the journey of learning any knowledge or skill—including combatting boredom.

- **Skills:** Finally, the skill set to avoid boredom is not something that develops naturally in children. It requires learning and practice, and this practice can even begin in infancy. Specific ways to offset the dull, tired, or bored experience can be modeled by adults, but the goal is for children to discover for themselves what helps them feel less bored.

HOW TO SPOT BOREDOM IN CHILDREN OF VARIOUS AGES

Infants: Boredom in a baby is quite different from boredom in older children. Babies *can* get bored, but their boredom is often a result of the biological, even instinctual need for emotional, cognitive, and physical stimulation. Babies are highly curious, and can usually entertain themselves by looking around, playing with their toes, and so on. If an infant cries, acts irritable, or seems restless, introducing a new toy, providing a comforting hug, or doing a new activity usually shifts the infant's distress if boredom is the reason behind it.

Toddlers: Toddlers, like babies, tend to be very busy and curious, and while they can get tired, irritable, and fatigued, they seldom get bored. However, like infants, toddlers need input or structure from others to provide the necessary stimulation because they don't have the language or cognition to be more independent yet. When they do experience boredom, it may be because they need a suggestion or guidance from an adult to try something new or engage in an activity. It's also helpful to check in with toddlers to see if behaviors that may look like boredom are really communicating something else. Is the child hungry? Tired? Seeking attention? Could the child be feeling unwell? On the relatively rare occasion when a child this age *is* genuinely bored, it's usually displayed with irritability, temper tantrums, or whiny demands.

Preschool-age children: This is the age at which boredom begins to root. Likewise, this is a pivotal developmental period in helping children identify and negotiate feelings of boredom. When parents and caregivers take the time to teach preschoolers cognitive strategies, encourage autonomy, and model problem-solving behaviors, a sense of agency begins to take root in little ones. When children in this age group find time on their hands, their boredom may present as irritability, crankiness, tearfulness, or clinginess. As with toddlers, it's helpful to check to see that a child's boredom isn't signaling something more, like basic needs for food, sleep, or comfort.

School-age children: Children in this age group feel bored more than infants, toddlers, and preschoolers. Also, boredom may now be reported both at home and at school. School-age children convey their frustration and displeasure quite well. Often, adults will hear statements like "I'm bored," "There's nothing to do," "This homework is stupid," "I hate school," and so on. Children this age also tend to be physically expressive with bored feelings, often stomping, slamming, hitting, or throwing things. School-age children may also complain of aches and pains when they're bored. This occurs because they are not fully aware of how the stress of boredom presses on their bodies.

FIVE TIPS FOR ADULTS TO HELP REDUCE BOREDOM IN CHILDREN

When it comes to reducing boredom in children, the following strategies can be helpful.

- **Embrace boredom:** Encourage children to understand that feeling bored is a typical and healthy experience, and note that boredom is an opportunity for discovery. Help children view boredom as a signal to become curious about their unique needs, desires, and interests.

- **Spur wonder:** Support creativity and imagination in children. Help them find wonder and curiosity with statements like "Think about what you want to do" or "How can you use your imagination to create some fun?"

- **Be patient:** Many children are used to adults scheduling their time, so expect the shift from boredom to self-started decision-making to take some practice. Try not to solve a child's boredom. Instead, let the moment linger and offer empathetic phrases like "I know you will find something to do" or "It's hard when you don't know what to do next."

- **Model problem-solving behavior:** Let children see *you* experiencing boredom, and show them how you move from a moment of passivity to activity. Allow them to hear you express emotions like "Gee, I feel bored today," followed by solutions such as "I think I'm going to read a book."

- **Praise effort:** Learning how to use boredom as a starting point for deeper enjoyment is a skill set that requires trial and error and plenty of practice. So be sure to praise children for trying, for efforts that work, and also for ones that fall flat. Remind children that using time for self-reflection is a wonderful thing.

WHEN TO SEEK PROFESSIONAL HELP

Boredom—like any other emotion—is a natural part of life for children (and for adults too). However, if boredom is not easily remedied and becomes a persistent issue, it may lead to other challenges. Ongoing boredom in childhood can be linked to poor academic performance, low self-esteem, anxiety, and depression, as well as anger and aggression. Chronic boredom in little ones may also lead to eventual drug or alcohol abuse, lower job satisfaction, and overall lower quality of life and lower life satisfaction as adults.

In some cases, serious and lasting boredom may signal something more. Long-standing fatigue and listlessness can be symptoms of medical issues like anemia, diabetes, hypothyroidism or hyperthyroidism, and other conditions. If you are concerned about excessive boredom and your child, check in with your pediatrician for a full physical. Children who have difficulty regulating their thoughts and feelings and cannot get unstuck from boredom may also be experiencing beginning symptoms of anxiety, attention disorders, or depression. Consultation with a mental health professional can assess if these behaviors require more specific interventions and can help children feel better and lead meaningful, healthy lives.

RESOURCES FOR MORE INFORMATION AND SUPPORT

American Academy of Pediatrics aap.org

Association for Children's Mental Health acmh-mi.org

Child Mind Institute childmind.org

Children and Adults with Attention Deficit/Hyperactivity Disorder chadd.org

National Education Association nea.org

National Foster Parent Association nfpaonline.org

National Institute of Mental Health nimh.nih.gov

National Parenting Education Network npen.org

National PTA pta.org

Zero to Three zerotothree.org

ABOUT THE AUTHOR AND ILLUSTRATOR OF THE SOMETIMES WHEN COLLECTION

Deborah Serani, Psy.D., is an award-winning author and psychologist who has been in practice for thirty years. She is also a professor at Adelphi University. Dr. Serani is a go-to expert for psychological issues. Her writing on depression and trauma has been published in many academic journals, and her interviews can be found in *Newsday*, *Psychology Today*, *The Chicago Tribune*, *The New York Times*, *The Associated Press*, and affiliate radio programs at CBS and NPR, among others. She is also a TEDx speaker. Dr. Serani lives on Long Island, New York.

Kyra Teis is a children's book author-illustrator, a graphic novelist, and an avid sewer of costumes and clothing. She works in a cozy studio in central New York, which is crammed full of books and fabrics from all over the world. When she's not making art, you can find her and her husband cheering wildly at their two daughters' soccer games and musical theater productions.

Other Great Books from Free Spirit

Sometimes When I'm Mad
by Deborah Serani, Psy.D.,
illustrated by Kyra Teis

For ages 4-8. 40 pp.; HC; full-color;
8¼" x 9".

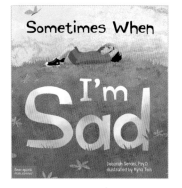

Sometimes When I'm Sad
by Deborah Serani, Psy.D.,
illustrated by Kyra Teis

For ages 4-8. 40 pp.; HC; full-color;
8¼" x 9".

I'm Happy-Sad Today
Making Sense of Mixed-Together Feelings
by Lory Britain, Ph.D., illustrated by Matthew Rivera

For ages 3–8. 40 pp.; HC; full-color; 11¼" x 9¼".

Step Back from Frustration
Kids Can Cope series
by Gill Hasson, illustrated by Sarah Jennings

For ages 6–9. 32 pp.; HC; full-color;
8¼" x 10½".

Waiting Is Not Forever
by Elizabeth Verdick,
illustrated by Marieka Heinlen

For ages 4–7. 40 pp.; PB; full-color;
9" x 9".

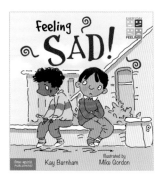

Feeling Sad!
by Kay Barnham,
illustrated by Mike Gordon

For ages 5–9. 32 pp.; HC; full-color;
7½" x 8¼".

Free Leader's Guide
freespirit.com/leader

Interested in purchasing multiple quantities and receiving volume discounts?
Contact edsales@freespirit.com or call 1.800.735.7323 and ask for Education Sales.

Many Free Spirit authors are available for speaking engagements, workshops, and keynotes.
Contact speakers@freespirit.com or call 1.800.735.7323.

For pricing information, to place an order, or to request a free catalog, contact:

Free Spirit Publishing Inc. • 6325 Sandburg Road • Suite 100 • Minneapolis, MN 55427-3674
toll-free 800.735.7323 • local 612.338.2068 • fax 612.337.5050 • help4kids@freespirit.com • freespirit.com